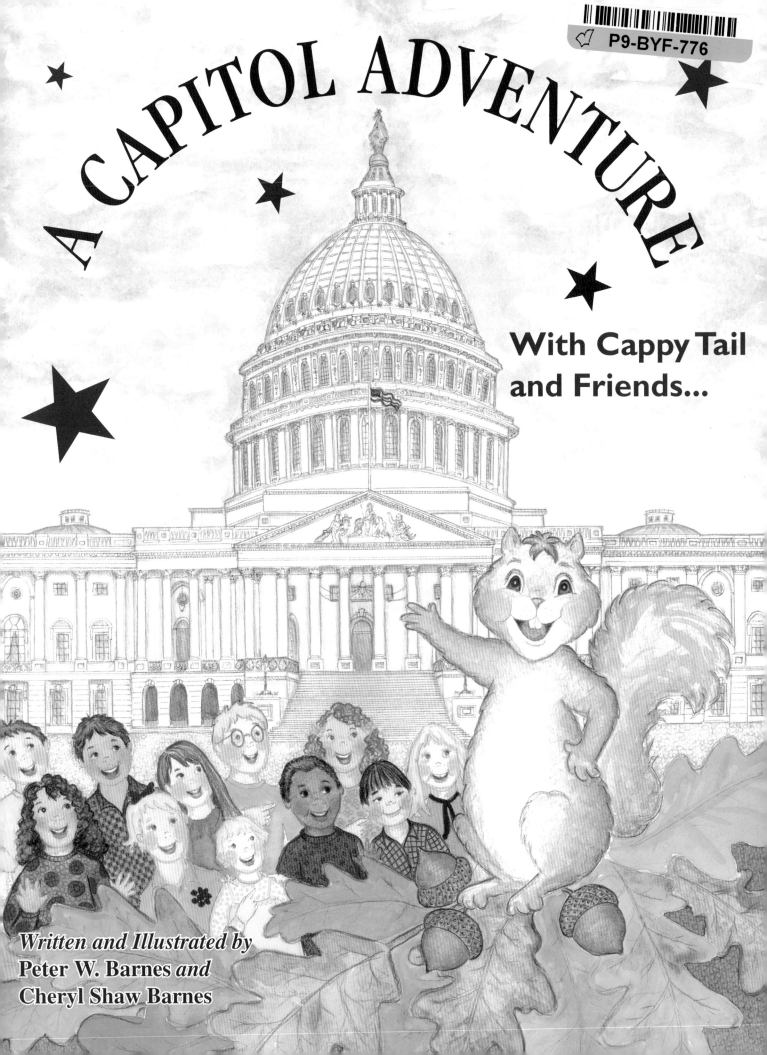

A CAPITOL ADVENTURE

With Cappy Tail and Friends...

Written and Illustrated by
Peter W. Barnes and
Cheryl Shaw Barnes

VSP Books

Go to **www.VSPBooks.com** today to get
autographed books and special discounts!

Contact us at **(800) 441-1949** or
e-mail us at **mail@VSPBooks.com** for more information

Copyright © 2010 by Peter W. Barnes and Cheryl Shaw Barnes

Design by Michele Charles Barnes

ISBN 978-1-893622-25-8

Library of Congress Catalog Card Number 2010925050

10 9 8 7 6 5 4 3 2 1

Printed in the United States of America

Look for these little critters in every illustration in this book!

Dedication

*This book is dedicated to the artist Constantino Brumidi (1805-1880),
who devoted much of the last 25 years of his life creating the masterpieces seen
throughout the Capitol. For his work, he has come to be known as
"The Michelangelo of the Capitol."*

*The Hulkower Family, dear friends: Mark (a champion of justice for all),
Nancy, Griffin, Annie and Maggie.*

*Our favorite little patriot and adopted granddaughter, Sarah Ayobi,
whose parents, John and Nazia, came to this country in search of a better life,
like so many others before them.*

— P.W.B. and C.S.B.

Acknowledgements

*Cappy and this book would have never come to life without the invaluable assistance of
the following people: Barbara Wolanin, Curator for the Architect of the Capitol;
Diane Skvarla, Curator, U.S. Senate; Melinda Smith, Associate Curator, U.S. Senate;
Maria Lopez, Deputy Clerk, U.S. House of Representatives; Farrar Elliott,
Curator and Chief, Office of History and Preservation, U.S. House of Representatives;
Chandini Bachman, of the U.S. Capitol Guide Service; and last but not least,
our friend Chuck Keyton, CVC Gift Shop Store Manager, who gave us the idea,
his patience and his inexhaustible support.*

Hi, my name is Cappy! I'm a special squirrel—you'll see!
Welcome the Capitol, in Washington, D.C.!
I'm so pleased you're visiting, so come and follow me
To learn about this monument to our democracy!

This shining building on a hill is more than just our nation's—
It's also been my family's home for many generations!
When President George Washington, in 1793,
Came here to lay the cornerstone, we watched him from this tree!

It's not every day, you know, that any boy or girl
Gets to have a conversation with a talking squirrel!
I know the Capitol so well—each nook and every cranny—
Some historians believe my knowledge is uncanny!

I'll scurry off this branch now so that I can be your guide—
Our journey of discovery begins with me, inside!
Our tour begins right over there—inside the door marked 'enter'—
A gateway to our history, the Capitol Visitors Center!

Emancipation Hall is where we start our exploration—
There's no charge or fee. And here's your only obligation:

Bring your curiosity—and your imagination!
Come along now! Step this way! Enjoy our presentation!

Look up there! The Capitol dome is set against the sky—
Rising 288 feet—and you thought my TREE was high!
There's our grand old flag! It proudly waves red, white and blue!
Fly away with me now and you'll learn a thing or two!

She waits patiently, nearby the information desk—
At 19-and-a-half feet tall, she's kind of—statuesque!
Statue of Freedom is her name and on the dome you'll see
Her twin sister, a towering symbol of our liberty.

In the room beyond, you'll find a helpful introduction
To the history of the Capitol and its construction.
Our Founding Fathers chose this site for its impressive view.
Down the years, these pictures show, the building grew and grew.

History of the Capitol

1793 Thornton design........Library of Congress

1. In 1793, Congress awarded an amateur architect, Dr. William Thornton, $500 and a building lot in the new federal city for his winning design of the Capitol. Dr. Thornton's inspiration came from a Roman temple, the Pantheon. George Washington and Thomas Jefferson selected Thornton's grand design.

1800 North wing /building.....Library of Congress

2. In 1800, the government moved from Philadelphia to its new home in Washington. The first building completed in the Capitol was the North Wing. The Senate, the House of Representatives and the Supreme Court all worked there. The North Wing housed the Library of Congress as well.

East Elevation of Capitol, 1804. Conjectural reconstruction, 1989.....Architect of the Capitol

3. As the young nation grew, it sent more representatives to Washington. In 1801, President Jefferson approved construction of this temporary brick building for the House of Representatives. It was known as "the Oven" because it looked like one on the outside and was very hot and stuffy on the inside. A 145-foot passageway connected "the Oven" to the North Wing.

Capitol burned by British 1814.......Kiplinger Washington Collection

4. Workers completed the South Wing, the permanent home of the House of Representatives, in 1808. During another war with the U.S., the British invaded Washington in 1814 and set fire to the new Capitol and other government buildings. By 1819, the reconstructed wings were complete and the Capitol reopened. The center building with its low dome was completed in 1824.

5. This is the earliest known photograph of the Capitol, taken in 1846 by John Plumbe, one of America's first commercial photographers. Architect Charles Bulfinch designed the low dome, which was made of brick, wood and copper.

1846 earliest know photograph.... Library of Congress

Low dome image of Capitol......The Athenaeum of Philadelphia

6. The nation continued to grow, sending even more lawmakers to Washington. They needed more space. Architect Thomas Ustick Walter designed extensions to the North and South, which more than doubled the size of the Capitol. This illustration shows Walter's proposed design with Bulfinch's existing low dome.

Walter's new design for dome. Library of Congress

7. Because Bulfinch's low dome looked out of proportion with Walter's new design, Walter proposed a new, taller dome. It was to be made of cast iron, which was lighter and cheaper than stone. Construction began in 1856, continued through the Civil War and was completed in 1865. Workers mounted the 19½-foot-tall bronze *Statue of Freedom* on the top in 1863.

Dome construction during Civil War...Architect of the Capitol

8. The new cast-iron dome was constructed with a steam-powered crane. During the Civil War, while workers assembled the dome, the Union Army temporarily used the Capitol as a barracks, hospital and bakery for soldiers.

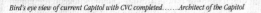
Bird's eye view of current Capitol with CVC completed......Architect of the Capitol

9. Over the years, architects and builders added other improvements to the Capitol and surrounding complex – a marble terrace for the Capitol, House and Senate office buildings, the Library of Congress, the Supreme Court and more. The Capitol Visitor Center opened under the East Plaza in 2008.

Brumidi's *The Apotheosis of Washington*

Italian-American artist Constantino Brumidi painted *The Apotheosis of Washington* in the Rotunda's ceiling, or canopy, in 1865. "Apotheosis" means "glorification of a person as an ideal." The painting covers 4,664 square feet. It shows our first president, George Washington, surrounded by 15 female figures. Thirteen of them represent the original states, one symbolizes "Liberty and Authority" and the other, "Victory and Fame." The surrounding scenes depict science, agriculture, commerce and other American capabilities.

Oak Leaves and Acorns

This ornate square is called a "coffer." There is a row of coffers located up the wall of the Rotunda and circling the room. See if you can find one of Cappy's cousins sitting in one of these coffers! Squirrels especially like oak leaves and acorns!

The Rotunda is magnificent, as anyone can see—
The paintings tell the story of our early history.
High above he sits, commanding over this great hall—
The Father of our Country, proudly watching over all!

Our nation's heroes populate the Statuary Hall.
Writers, teachers, soldiers and inventors line the wall.
When I whisper and you put your hand up to your ear,
It will carry clear across the room, as you can hear!

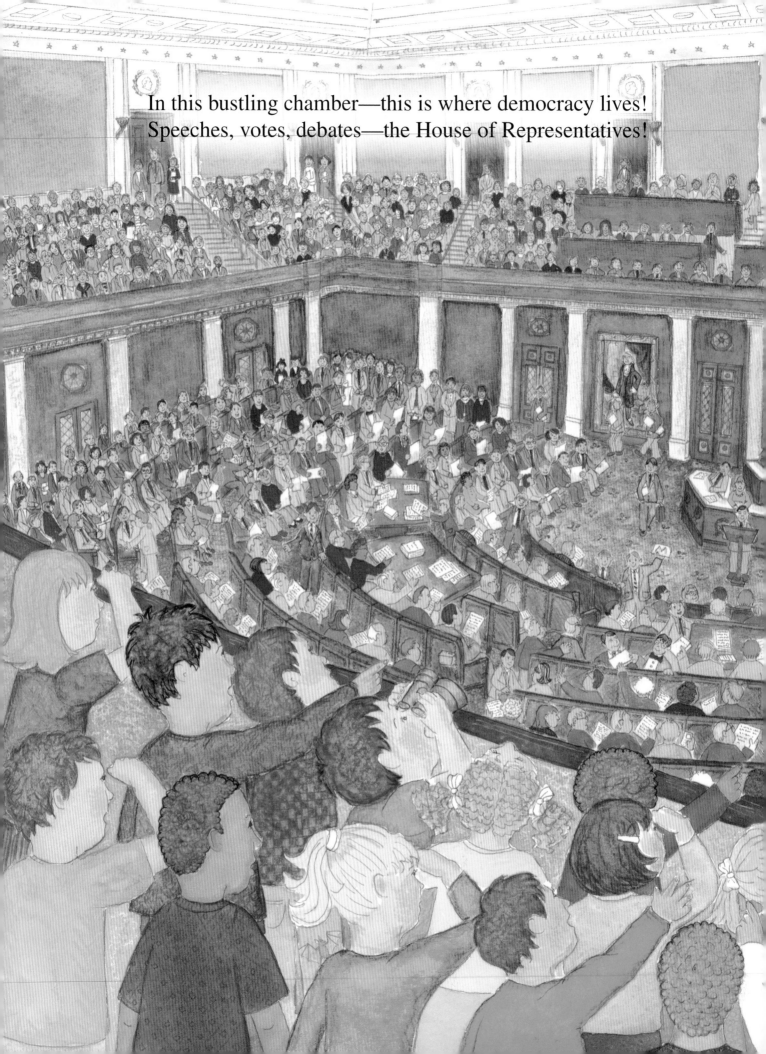

In this bustling chamber—this is where democracy lives!
Speeches, votes, debates—the House of Representatives!

Members, clerks and pages, in a legislative whirl—
Children, can you find a patriotic, talking squirrel?

Our Founding Fathers, when they wrote our cherished Constitution,
Established—with deliberation, care and resolution—
A special body to protect our liberties and laws,
For everybody—even those of us with tails and paws!

They called it the Supreme Court—this is where it used to meet.
(Now you'll find it in a building right across the street.)
Great judges known as "justices" met here, year after year,
Working to uphold the many freedoms we hold dear.

In this corridor, the walls and ceiling are so pretty,
Painted by one artist, the incomparable Brumidi!
He painted in the Capitol for more than 20 years.
Thank you, Constantino! Hooray for him! Three cheers!

"The greatest deliberative body in the world," as it is known—
Careful, thoughtful and reflective—that's the Senate's tone!

Senators respect tradition—into the "well" they stroll
To cast their votes each time they hear, "The clerk will call the roll!"

Welcome to the "The Crypt" – it is a room that sounds mysterious.
But to the building's architects, its purpose is quite serious—
The Rotunda sits above on tons of stone, you see—
The 40 massive columns here support it perfectly!

You will find a starburst right beneath the chandelier,
Pointing North, South, East and West, to all that we hold dear,
From the mountains to the prairies, from sea to shining sea,
The United States of America—the home of the brave and the free!

Well, our tour is done now and we hope that it has shown
The Capitol is more than just a building made of stone—
It's the people's place – our place! A place we all belong—
The living, breathing heart of our democracy, so strong!

All of us who work here, in the shadow of this dome,
Thank you for your visit and wish you safe travels home.
Now I'll scurry back inside and scurry down the hall—
Scurry to my secret quiet place right up the wall!

So until we meet again—God bless us one and all!

The Capitol Complex

Construction of the Capitol began in 1793 on land selected by our first president, George Washington, and Pierre Charles L'Enfant, the French-American engineer who designed the federal city. Lawmakers began meeting in the Capitol in 1800. Thomas Jefferson was the first president inaugurated there, in 1801. The park-like grounds around the Capitol cover 58.8 acres planted with more than 100 varieties of trees and bushes, as well as thousands of seasonal garden flowers. And—it is home to a lot of squirrels! The grounds were landscaped by renowned landscape architect Frederick Law Olmsted, who also designed Central Park in New York City.

The Capitol Visitor Center

The Capitol Visitor Center, located between Constitution and Independence Avenues under the East Plaza, is a welcome center providing information and education for all who come to the Capitol. Visitors can view extraordinary exhibits highlighting the growth of the Capitol and Congress. Construction began in 2002 and the CVC opened in 2008. At 580,000 square feet spread over three levels underground, it is the largest expansion of the Capitol ever undertaken. Excavation workers removed 65,000 truckloads of soil to make space for the CVC. In its first year, it welcomed 2.3 million visitors.

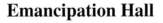

Emancipation Hall

In 2007, Congress approved legislation naming the central space of the Capitol Visitor Center "Emancipation Hall" to recognize the contribution of enslaved laborers who helped to build the Capitol. Tour guides meet the visitors who enter here. The room features a plaster model for the *Statue of Freedom* and busts of two people who fought against oppression. The hall also houses 18 statues of historic figures donated by various states. Two theaters provide visitors with an orientation film; two smaller theaters broadcast proceedings of the Senate and House of Representatives. The Exhibition Hall shows the history, expansion and development of the Capitol and the Congress. The displays include original artifacts and historical documents.

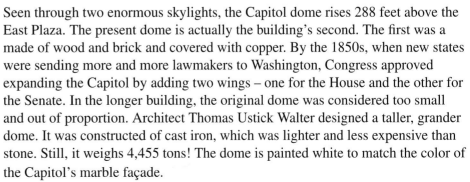

The Capitol Dome

Seen through two enormous skylights, the Capitol dome rises 288 feet above the East Plaza. The present dome is actually the building's second. The first was a made of wood and brick and covered with copper. By the 1850s, when new states were sending more and more lawmakers to Washington, Congress approved expanding the Capitol by adding two wings – one for the House and the other for the Senate. In the longer building, the original dome was considered too small and out of proportion. Architect Thomas Ustick Walter designed a taller, grander dome. It was constructed of cast iron, which was lighter and less expensive than stone. Still, it weighs 4,455 tons! The dome is painted white to match the color of the Capitol's marble façade.

The *Statue of Freedom*

This 19½-foot plaster model was used to create the mold for casting the bronze *Statue of Freedom* that sits atop the dome. American sculptor Thomas Crawford designed it in 1856. Crawford chose a classic female figure to represent "armed Freedom triumphant in war and peace." She holds a sword, shield and victory wreath; her headdress is composed of the head of an eagle, feathers and stars. The finished statue was mounted on the dome in 1863. Crawford designed other sculpture and works of art for the Capitol, including the bronze doors for the House and Senate featuring scenes from American history.

The Rotunda

The Rotunda is located in the center of the Capitol. It is 96 feet wide and 180 feet high. The circular room is decorated with eight large paintings. Four of them, by artist John Trumbull, depict scenes from the Revolutionary War. Statues and a frieze (paintings that look like stone sculpture in a "belt" around the room starting 58 feet above the floor) honor important people and events in American history. The *Apotheosis of Washington*, celebrating our first president, George Washington, is the painting on the curved ceiling, or canopy. The Rotunda is used for Congressional ceremonies and to honor presidents and other important people who have died.

National Statuary Hall

This large, semi-circular room was originally the meeting place for the House of Representatives. Seven members who served here went on to become president. After the House moved to its new wing in 1857, Congress voted to preserve the two-story chamber as a "National Statuary Hall." Congress invited each state to contribute two marble or bronze statues of its most prominent citizens. The first statue arrived in 1870. Eventually, there were so many statues that Congress agreed to spread them around the Capitol. The room is also a unique "whispering gallery"—whispers at one end of it can be heard clearly at the other end. Formerly known as the Old Hall of the House, it is still used for ceremonies and special occasions, including presidential luncheons.

The House of Representatives

The "People's House" began meeting in this chamber in 1857. Under the Constitution, each state elects representatives based on population – if a state has more citizens, it gets to elect more representatives (but each state gets at least one). To stand for election, a representative must be at least 25 years old and have been an American citizen for at least seven years. House members serve two-year terms. During that time, they write, debate and vote on legislation that—if approved by the Senate and signed by the president—becomes our nation's laws. In the early days, each member sat at a desk. But the nation grew so big that the increasing number of representatives began to crowd the room. Congress eventually capped membership at 435 representatives, who now sit on long benches.

The Old Supreme Court Chamber

When our Founding Fathers wrote the Constitution and Bill of Rights, they created a special body – the Supreme Court – to uphold the nation's fundamental laws, such as the right to free speech and freedom of religion for all citizens. The highest court in the land, the Court is made up of nine very smart, very wise people called "justices." The area where this room is now located was originally used as the chamber for the Senate. President Thomas Jefferson was inaugurated there in 1801 and 1805. Architect Benjamin Henry Latrobe thought it was appropriate to create a two-story Senate chamber on the same level as the House chamber. The Supreme Court Chamber, with its columns, archways and vaulted ceilings, was built below the Senate Chamber. The court met here from 1819 to 1860. Each justice selected his own chair. The justices heard and decided many historic, "landmark" cases in this room.

The Brumidi Corridor

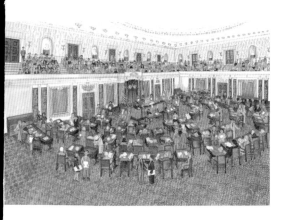

An immigrant from Italy, Constantino Brumidi was known as the "Artist of the Capitol" for the work he did here for over 25 years. The Brumidi Corridor, located on the Senate side of the Capitol, is adorned with intricate, colorful murals he and his team of artists painted from 1857 to 1859. Along with portraits and images of classical and historic figures, Brumidi painted plants, birds, insects and animals indigenous to the United States. A bust of Brumidi is located in this corridor. The richly patterned floor tiles were made by a renowned English tile company of the time, Minton, Hollins & Co. These elaborate tiles are also found in other parts of the Capitol.

The Senate

As our country added more states, two new wings for the Capitol were approved to make room for all of the new senators and House members. Located in the North Wing, this grand chamber was used for the first time in 1859. Under the Constitution, each state elects two senators. A senator must be at least 30 years old and have been a U.S. citizen for at least nine years. Senators are elected to six-year terms. Like members of the House, senators write, debate and vote on legislation. While members of the House no longer sit at desks, the Senate still uses antique desks for its members. Some of them are famous— many are the same ones made after British soldiers burned the Capitol in 1814. One desk in the back row even has a drawer full of candy!

The Crypt

A crypt is usually an underground chamber. But the Crypt at the Capitol is a circular room on the first floor that is now used to display sculpture. It also serves an important architectural purpose—it lies one floor below the Rotunda. The Crypt's 40 columns support the Rotunda's heavy stone floor. There is a starburst embedded in the center in the Crypt's floor. It marks the point from which all the streets of Washington are laid out and numbered.

The East Plaza

Our story ends on the Capitol's East Plaza. From there, visitors can tour other landmarks nearby, including House and Senate office buildings. Just across the street on the left is the Supreme Court building; the Court moved there from the Capitol in 1935. On the right is the Library of Congress; the library also once resided in the Capitol. Completed in 1897, the building is named for President Jefferson. His personal collection of 6,487 books restocked the library after the British burned the Capitol – and the books within—in 1814. Today, the Library of Congress is home to more than 130 million items, including more than 29 million cataloged books and other printed materials.

Squirrel Painting

As for a certain talking squirrel, our Cappy Tail was inspired by this image in a Brumidi wall mural located near the Patent Corridor in the Senate wing of the Capitol. Brumidi painted many squirrels, mice, birds, butterflies, beetles and other creatures in this corridor. Capitol Hill is home to many squirrels. Like most people, we are nuts about them!

Constantino Brumidi (1805-1880)

Constantino Brumidi called himself "The Artist of the Capitol" but came to be known as "The Michelangelo of the Capitol." Born in Rome, Brumidi studied painting and sculpture as a young man and painted frescos at the Vatican and in Roman palaces. Fresco is a difficult technique: the artist brushes pigments mixed with water directly on to wet plaster. As the plaster dries and cures, the colors become part of the wall. As a result, the artist must work quickly, painting each section of plaster on the day it is applied. Ancient Roman and Italian Renaissance artists inspired Brumidi, especially the work of Raphael. In 1852, at 47 years old, Brumidi emigrated to the U.S. to look for jobs painting murals in churches. He began painting in the Capitol in 1855 and spent a lot of time working there until his death in 1880.

Bibliography

Allen, William C. *History of the United States Capitol, A chronicle of design, construction, and politics.* Washington, D.C.: U.S. Government Printing Office, 2001

—. *The Dome of the United States Capitol: An Architectural History.* Washington, D.C.: U.S. Government Printing Office, 1992.

—. *The United States Capitol: A Brief Architectural History.* Washington, D.C.: U.S. Government Printing Office, 1990.

Berard, Jim. *The Capitol Inside & Out.* Marshall, Va.: EPM Publications, 2003

Brown, Glenn. *History of the United States Capitol.* Introduction and annotations by William B. Bushong. Washington, D.C.: U.S. Government Printing Office, 2007

Dodge, Andrew. *A Young Person's Guide to the United States Capitol.* Washington, D.C.: The United States Capitol Historical Society, 2000.

Maroon, Fred J. and Suzy Maroon. *The United States Capitol.* New York: Stewart, Tabori & Chang, 1993.

Reed, Henry Hope. *The United States Capitol, Its Architecture and Decoration.* New York: W.W. Norton, 2005.

U.S. Capitol Historical Society, *We, the People: The Story of the United States Capitol, Its Past and Its Promise.* Washington, D.C.: U.S. Capitol Historical Society, 2002

U.S. Senate. *United States Senate Catalogue of Fine Art.* Washington, D.C.: U.S. Government Printing Office, 2002.

Wolanin, Barbara A. *Constantino Brumidi*: *Artist of the Capitol.* Washington, D.C.: U.S. Government Printing Office, 1998.

Online Resources

Architect of the Capitol, www.aoc.gov

Library of Congress, www.loc.gov

U.S. Capitol Historical Society, www.uschs.org

U.S. Capitol Visitor Center, www.visitthecapitol.gov

U.S. Senate, www.senate.gov

U.S. House of Representatives, www.house.gov

U.S. Supreme Court, www.supremecourtus.gov

VSP Books

Woodrow for President
Teaches children about voting,
elections and good citizenship.
In rhyming verse.
Grades K-4. ISBN 1-893622-01-0

Woodrow, the White House Mouse
Tells the story of the job of the president
and the art, architecture and history
of the White House through rhyming verse.
Grades K-4. ISBN 0-9637688-9-1

House Mouse, Senate Mouse
Teaches children how our laws are
made in our nation's Capitol.
In rhyming verse, grades K-4.
ISBN 0-9637688-4-0

**Marshall, the
Courthouse Mouse**
Teaches children how the Supreme Co
protects our consitution. In rhyming ve
Grades 1-5. ISBN 0-9637688-6-7

Nat, Nat, the Nantucket Cat
Takes children on a tour of beautiful
Nantucket Island, Massachusetts.
Grades K-2. In rhyming verse.
ISBN 0-9637688-0-8

**Nat, Nat, the Nantucket
Cat Goes to the Beach**
Nat explores Nantucket's beaches.
Preschool and grades K-2.
Rhyming verse, ISBN 1-893622-05-3

Where's Nat?
Find Nat hidden in the illustrations of
the special places and events in Nantucket.
Preschool to grade 3. Rhyming verse.
ISBN 1-893622-19-3

Little Miss Patriot
Marion learns about civics and
helping her community and country.
Available in generic and NFRW editio
Grades 1-4. ISBN 1-893622-20-7

Cornelius Vandermouse
Teaches children about historic
Newport, Rhode Island.
Grades K-4. ISBN 0-9637688-5-9

**Mizner Mouse,
the Pride of Palm Beach**
Takes children on a tour of Palm Beach.
Ages 5-8. ISBN 1-893622-12-6

Washington, DC ABC's
An alphabet and picture book
celebrating Washington's history,
events, people and places.
Grades 1-6. ISBN 1-893622-06-1

**Alexander, the Old
Town Mouse**
Teaches children about historic
Alexandria, Virginia.
Grades K-3. ISBN 09637688-1-6

President Adams' Alligator
Teaches children about the
presidents through their pets.
Grades 1-4. ISBN 1-893622-13-4

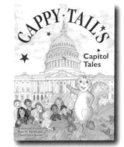

Cappy Tail's Capitol Tales
Cappy Tail takes children on a
tour of our U.S. Capitol.
Grades 1-6. ISBN 1-893622-22-7

**Virginia: An Alphabetical
Journey Through History**
An alphabet and picture book teaching
children about the Old Dominion.
Grades 3-5, ISBN 1893622-14-2

Maestro Mouse
Teaches children about the National
Symphony Orchestra and its
instruments at the the Kennedy Cente
in Washington, D.C.
Grades K-3, ISBN 1-893622-17-7

www.VSPBooks.com